# The
# Upside-Down
# Gardener

In memory of

Dorothy Parchinsky, a lady who taught me
how to bloom and grow forever

— C.S.

My thanks to
Malinda
for being fun to draw.

— P.A.

# The Upside-Down Gardener

### A Dory Oslo Adventure

## Chrysa Smith

## Illustrations by Pat Achilles

THE WELL BRED BOOK

# Introduction

Do you know how much fun it can be to plant a seed?
When those first tiny baby plants appear, it is so
exciting. You add soil. And water. And sun. It's magic!
Well, sometimes it all turns upside down. That's what
happened to Dory Oslo. And this is her story.

— *Chrysa Smith*

"I'm freezing," said Dory.

"Well, it is starting to warm up a little," said Dory's mom.

"You know, Mom," said Dory, "people smile more when it's warm. They wear bright colors. They play baseball!"

"I know you are ready for spring, honey. I can see that you want to get on that field. But we do need to raise some money for your new uniforms. We'll have to work on that. For now, maybe we can add some of those bright colors to our own world."

"How are we going to do that?" Dory asked.

"You and I can plant our very own garden."

"Me, a gardener?" Dory asked.

"Why not you, Dory?" her mother said, "All you have to do is plant a seed."

When they got home, Dory's mom showed her pictures of beautiful gardens. Then her mom grabbed her gloves, some seed packets and a watering can.

"Come on, honey," Mom said. "Let's go have a look in our yard."

As they stepped outside, Dory looked at the big brick buildings. She saw the trash cans and a few cats in the alley behind their house. And she saw only a small piece of the sun. Dory wondered how a garden could ever grow in this tiny backyard. But her mom took the shovel and dug up some dirt.

"Open the seed packets," she told Dory, "and sprinkle those seeds into the soil. Now cover them with more soil. Water them. And wait."

"I'm not very good at waiting," said Dory.

"Well then, this may be the perfect project for you," Mom said.

Dory thought about those tiny seeds. How were they going to turn into beautiful flowers? Could this little garden be filled with color? She couldn't wait to see what it would look like tomorrow.

But tomorrow came and the little garden looked the
same. Dory thought, *When my mom wants to wake up, she
uses her alarm clock.*

So Dory ran upstairs and got her mom's alarm clock. She
placed it in the garden and pressed a button that would make
it ring.

"Come on, plants. Wake up!" Dory yelled.

But the little seeds just sat there in the ground.

The next day, the little garden still looked the same.
Dory thought, *My dad says nothing wakes him up like a
good cup of coffee.*

So Dory took the pot of coffee from her kitchen and poured it over the entire garden.

"Come on, plants," Dory shouted, "Wake up!"

But the little seeds just sat there in the ground.

On the third day, the little garden looked the same. Dory thought, *When my baseball coach wants his players to wake up, he blows a whistle.*

So Dory went to her bag of baseball gear and dug down deep to find a whistle. She brought it outside and blew it so hard, her cheeks turned red.

"Come on, plants," Dory yelled, "Wake up! I want to see all of your colors."

But the little seeds just sat there in the ground.

"I knew this garden was a dumb idea," Dory said. "All I want is to be warm. I want to see bright colors. I want to see people smile. And I want to get my bright new uniform and finally play baseball!"

Dory thought about all of those pictures her mother showed her of beautiful flowers. She would love to grow flowers like that, but it didn't look like that was going to happen.

That night, Dory went to her room, sat down and closed her eyes. She thought about beautiful flowers coming up in her little city yard. She thought about getting new uniforms and she wondered how it would all get done.

Just then, Dory heard her mom yell, "Honey, come over here. I can't believe it! Plants have sprouted all over the garden."

Dory joined her mom at the back door. There in the little garden patch were pale branches poking out of the dirt. "Those don't look like your pictures, Mom. Did we do something wrong?"

Sirens wailed from the street out front, so Dory and her mom went to investigate. They were surprised to see a huge crowd gathered around their subway station and the police directing traffic. The sidewalk was jammed with news crews and their microphones, lights and cameras.

"What's going on?" Dory asked her neighbor.

"There are flowers growing in the subway! It's so exciting. There are plants growing on the ceiling, down the walls. We've never seen anything like it."

Dory's mom said, "Oh my. Maybe there's a school project going on. Someone is always trying to make the city look more beautiful. That must be it."

"Oh no," their neighbor said, "Children wouldn't be allowed to work down there in the subway. It is way too dangerous. I think it's a garden club."

"Quiet, please!" yelled a man wearing a headset and TV news jacket. "We're going on the air in five, four, three, two, one…"

A woman with a microphone spoke, "This is TV-Three News at the scene of a spring miracle. Overnight, this little neighborhood subway station has turned into a flowering paradise. No one knows how the plants got here, or how they are able to grow upside-down."

The crowd murmured about the strange upside-down garden, and Dory got to thinking about her own strange-looking plants.

"Mom, you know how my new plants look funny?" Dory's mom nodded. "They are all stems and branches."

"Right," Dory said as they returned to their yard. "Where are the leaves?"

"They look like roots!" Mom said.

"Aren't roots supposed to grow down, not up?" Dory asked.

"Usually," her mom said. "What do you say? Should we pick one and see what's happening?"

So they dug around the stem of one plant. And as they dug down a little farther, Dory's eyes got as big as sunflowers, and so did her mom's. They found flowers with pink and green dots. Flowers with red and yellow stripes. Big flowers with little blue flowers inside of them!

"I think this might be where the subway flowers came from," Dory said, "but I don't know why."

Dory's mom threw back her head and laughed. "All your funny ways of trying to wake up your plants must have scared them so much, they grew upside down! I think that you have just become the world's first upside-down gardener!"

Just as Dory was about to run out front to tell the reporters what they had discovered, she felt someone shaking her. Her mom said, "Come on. Wake up, sweetheart. It's time to eat dinner!"

"Dinner?" Dory sat up and rubbed her eyes. "Where are the reporters and the cameras?"

Dory told her mom all about their yard full of roots and how she scared her plants so much they grew down instead of up, and filled the subway station with big, beautiful flowers.

"Oh, Dory," her mom said, "you have some wild dreams."

"It was all a dream?" Dory asked. "You mean my plants didn't grow?"

"Part of it was a dream. But if you look outside, you will see that little green stems have popped up all over the garden." Her mom said. "Whatever pops up, it will still make people smile."

"I had a thought," Dory said. "If we can make people smile, do you think they can do that for us, too?"

"What do you mean, honey?"

"I was thinking that if we share our food and flowers, maybe people would donate some money for our new baseball uniforms." Dory said.

"That's a great idea, honey," said her mom. "Even better than alarm clocks and coffee and whistles in the garden."

"Well, Dory," her mom said. "Even though you didn't grow giant striped flowers upside down, you have shared beautiful, living things and made people smile. And you have raised a good bit of money. I think you are something even better than an upside-down gardener. You are a good and kind person."

"Thanks, Mom," said Dory, waving as she walked away.

Mom called, "Where are you going, Dory?"

"Where else?" she said. "I'm going to baseball practice and get my new uniform."

# More Books by Chrysa Smith

The Adventures of
the Poodle Posse Series:

1. *The Case of the Missing Steak Bone/
Who Let the Dogs Out?*

2. *The Princess and the Frenchmen/
No Dogs Allowed!*

3. *Creepy Tails!*

4. *Trouble Down Under*

5. *A Very Merry, Mixed-Up Christmas*

Once upon a Poodle
*A Picture Book*

Available at
The Lahaska Bookshop, Peddler's Village, PA
The Doylestown Bookshop, Doylestown, PA
The Newtown Bookshop, Newtown, PA
www.wellbredbook.net
Amazon


# See more artwork by Pat Achilles at

### www.AchillesPortfolio.com

*Published by The Well Bred Book:*
**www.wellbredbook.net**

**Chrysa Smith** is a lifetime writer and author of the award-winning, transitional series, *The Adventures of the Poodle Posse*, picture book *Once upon a Poodle* and her first almost non-canine tale, *The Upside-Down Gardener.*

**Pat Achilles** is an illustrator and cartoonist for children's books, greeting cards and magazines, and co-founder of the Bucks County Illustrators Society. She writes about drawing and sketching on her blog, *Pencilled In*, which is on her website AchillesPortfolio.com.

**Laurel Garver** is a Philadelphia-based editor who enjoys word games, Celtic music, and quirky indie films. She is the author of two novels, *Never Gone* and *Almost There*, and a poetry collection, *Muddy-Fingered Midnights.* She blogs at laurelgarver.blogspot.com.

12801753R00024

Made in the USA
Middletown, DE
18 November 2018